WHAT'S WRONG HERE?

By
Tony Tallarico

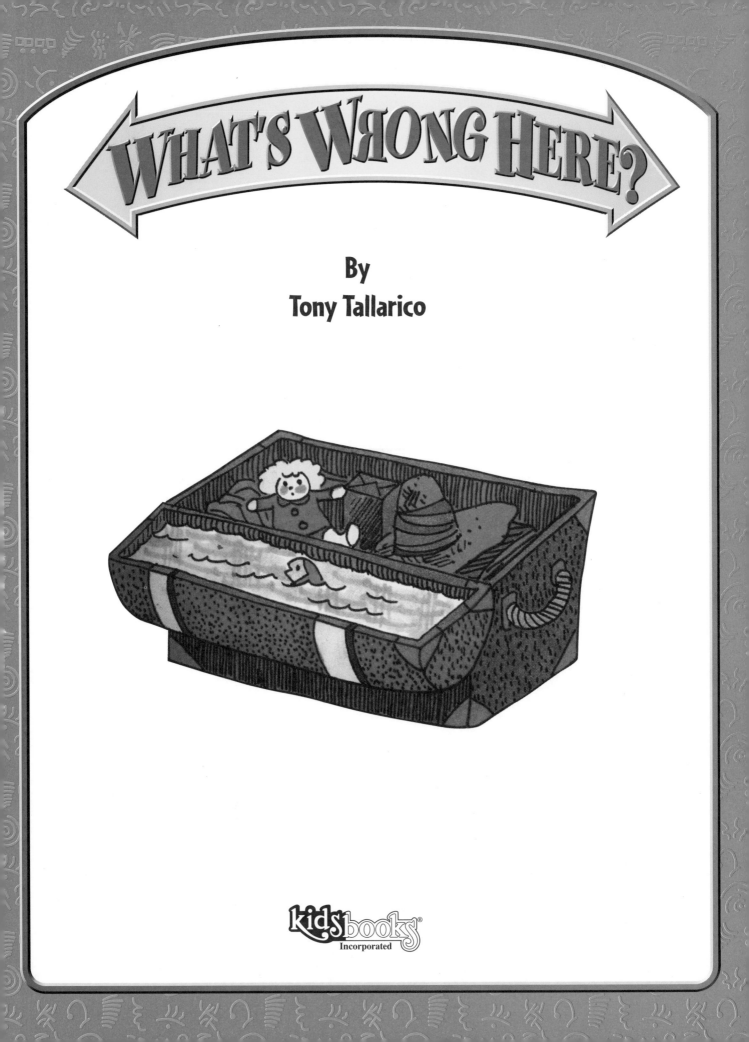

kidsbooks
Incorporated

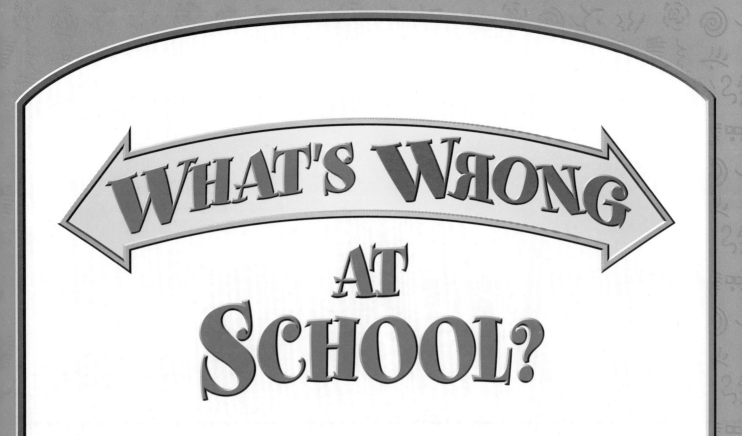

WHAT'S WRONG

AT
SCHOOL?

Answers on page 26

Monday morning. A new week of school begins with an enjoyable bus ride through town. Before the students arrive at school, can you find at least 13 things that are wrong with this picture?

The first lesson of the day is arithmetic. But what's wrong here? Search for and find at least <u>12</u> things that are wrong in this classroom.

The annual school play is scheduled to begin in a few days. However, there are a few things wrong with this full-dress rehearsal. Look for exactly 10 of them.

12

13

The Arts and Crafts Club is meeting in room 221. Everything is under control—or is it? Find at least 12 things that are out of control and wrong with this picture.

Lunchtime! The students can't wait to dig into all that great food! Seek and find at least <u>13</u> things that are wrong in this lunchroom.

Today is the day of the big test. Exams aren't really that difficult if you've studied for them. If you haven't, you'll have many wrong answers. Can you find <u>12</u> things that are wrong here?

This year, the class trip is to Prehistoric Times Amusement Park. The dinosaur slide looks like fun! Find at least 15 things wrong with this picture.

23

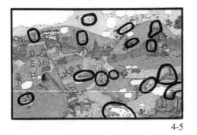

4-5

6-7

8-9

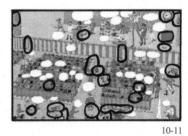

10-11

12-13

14-15

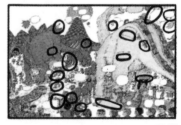

16-17

18-19

20-21

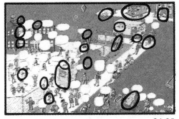

22-23

24-25

WHAT'S WRONG

IN THE
HAUNTED
HOUSE?

Answers on page 50

The children have discovered a real haunted house! Who's going to be brave enough to enter? You'll find out on the next page. But first, what's wrong here? At least 15 things. Can you find them?

29

Everyone is afraid to enter the house except Bob and Bobbie. Before they open the front door, find at least <u>15</u> things that are wrong with this picture.

All the children follow Bob and Bobbie into the house. In the living room they see 13 ghosts! First find them. Then try to find at least 6 things that are wrong with this picture.

TICK-TOCK-TICK-TOCK!

CAP

34

36

A giant skeleton drops in on the kids! Every scared one of them scrambles to get out. Before they do, search for and find at least 10 things that are wrong with this picture.

38

41

Bob and Bobbie gather their friends together for a meeting. The creatures in the house all seem to be hungry. Before the children share their milk and cookies, find at least 12 things that are wrong in this picture.

43

After snack time, the creatures and the children decide to play some games. Seek and find at least <u>10</u> wrong things here before they play Hide and Seek.

45

The friendly fiends ask the children to help them fix and clean the haunted house. Look at the mess in this room and find at least **10** things that are wrong.

47

The house is soon fixed, cleaned, and painted, both inside and out. It looks so good that no one will ever believe it was a genuine haunted house. We know better! But there are still at least 10 wrong things here for you to find.

28-29

30-31

32-33

34-35

36-37

38-39

40-41

42-43

44-45

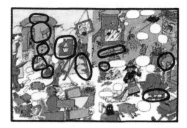

46-47

48-49

What's Wrong

at the Amusement Park?

Answers on page 74

The first stop is the Wacky Little Schoolhouse. Come inside and help find at least <u>10</u> things that are wrong here.

The flume ride is almost ready to go—except for a few things that are wrong. Can you find exactly 12 things that are wrong with this picture?

No amusement park is complete without its very own wacky circus. How many wrong things can you find here?

THIS IS THE GREAT WACKY CIRCUS!

59

Welcome to the wildest roller coaster ever! Besides the thrills and chills, there are <u>10</u> things wrong with this ride for you to find.

Have your tickets ready, please! The Toot-Toot train ride has begun. Along the way, look for and find at least 18 things that are wrong with this picture.

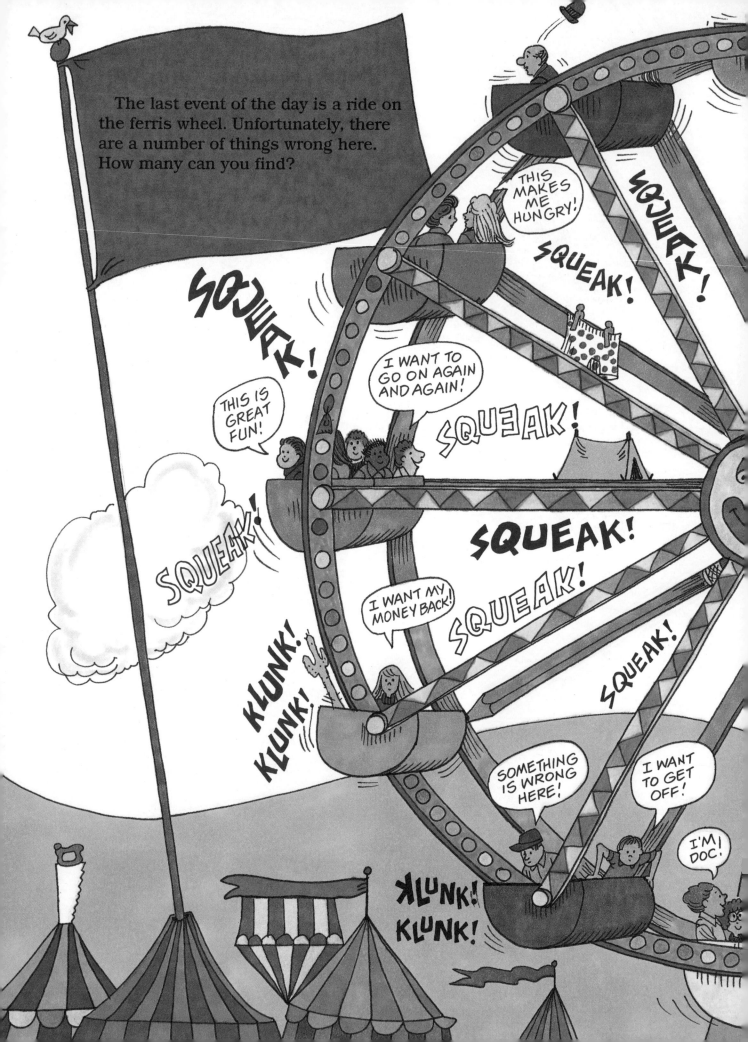

The last event of the day is a ride on the ferris wheel. Unfortunately, there are a number of things wrong here. How many can you find?

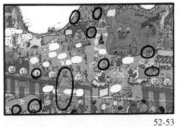

52-53

54-55

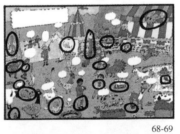

56-57

58-59

60-61

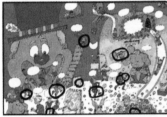

62-63

64-65

66-67

68-69

70-71

72-73

WHAT'S WRONG AT THE MOVIES?

Answers on page 96

It's movie time! Let's all go see our favorite flick! But first, find at least <u>12</u> things that are wrong with this picture.

The time is 1849. The place is the American West. The movie studio has spent $100,000,000 to make this film as accurate as possible. However, 11 wrong things have slipped past the director. Can you find them?

The Ninjas are getting ready to do battle on the big screen—and you are seeing it! Can you also see 10 things that are wrong with this picture?

The great detective Sheerluck Homes is featured in his 249th movie. The old boy is searching for that famous criminal, Professor Moranutty. What he *should* be searching for is all the things that are wrong in this picture. How many can you find?

SHERELUCK IS AT HIS BEST!

HE WENT TO SCHOOL WITH MY GRANDFATHER!

A typical day in space. As the spacecraft approaches the planet Sha-Quab, an astronaut drops in for a visit. But suddenly, 10 wrong things appear in this picture. Your mission is to find them!
THAT PLANET IS A GIANT BALLOON!
I'M GLAD I'M NOT IN THIS FILM!
ME TOO!
THIS IS AWFUL!
THIS MAKES ME SEE SICK!
I LIKE IT!
PLEASE KEEP YOUR HAT ON!
WHO WROTE THIS STORY?
NO ONE!
I ALREADY SAW THIS ON TV!
I DON'T WANT TO SEE THIS!
I'M GOING HOME!

Hurry up and sit down! The monster movie has begun. But before you are too comfortably settled in your seat, take a good look and find what's wrong here: exactly **13** things.

Today's cartoon feature is *Honey Bunny Goes Planting.* A few things have gone wrong here. Can you find at least 10 of them?

Grunt—the movie everyone has been waiting for—is now playing at your favorite theater. It's about the world's longest marathon. There are at least 13 things wrong with this race for you to find.

93

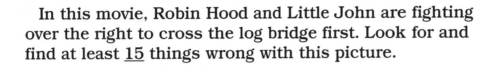

In this movie, Robin Hood and Little John are fighting over the right to cross the log bridge first. Look for and find at least 15 things wrong with this picture.

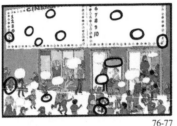

76-77

78-79

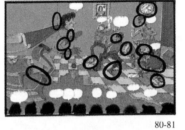

80-81

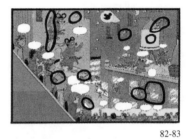

82-83

84-85

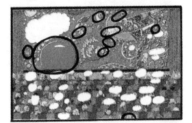

86-87

88-89

90-91

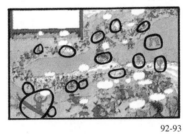

92-93

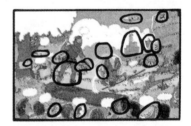

94-95